How do I use this scheme?

Key Words with Peter and Jane has three parallel series, each containing twelve books. All three series are written using the same carefully controlled vocabulary. Readers will get the most out of **Key Words** with Peter and Jane when they follow the books in the pattern 1a, 1b, 1c; 2a, 2b, 2c and so on.

• Series a
gradually introduces and repeats new words.

• Series b
provides further practice of these same words, but in a different context and with different illustrations.

• Series c
uses familiar words to teach **phonics** in a methodical way, enabling children to read increasingly difficult words. It also provides a link to writing.

Published by Ladybird Books Ltd
A Penguin Company
Penguin Books Ltd., 80 Strand, London WC2R 0RL, UK
Penguin Books Australia Ltd, 707 Collins Street, Melbourne, Victoria 3008, Australia
Penguin Group (NZ) 67 Apollo Drive, Rosedale, North Shore 0632, New Zealand

034

ISBN: 978-1-40930-111-0

Printed in China

Key Words

with Peter and Jane

1a Play with us

written by W. Murray
illustrated by J.H. Wingfield

Peter   Jane

a dog   a tree   a ball

toys   a shop

Peter

Jane

a dog

a tree

a ball

toys

a shop

Peter

Peter

Jane

Jane

Peter and Jane

---

new word

and

here is Peter

and

here is Jane

---

here   is

Peter is here

and

Jane is here.

---

no new words

Here is

the dog.

Here   the   dog

Here is Jane and here is the dog.

Jane likes
the dog
and
Peter likes
the dog.

---

new word

likes

The dog likes Jane and the dog likes Peter.

The

I like Peter.

I

I like Jane.

I like

the dog.

Here is

a shop.

---

new words

a   shop

Here is
a toy shop.
I like
the toy shop

---

new word

toy

Peter is in
the toy shop

---

in

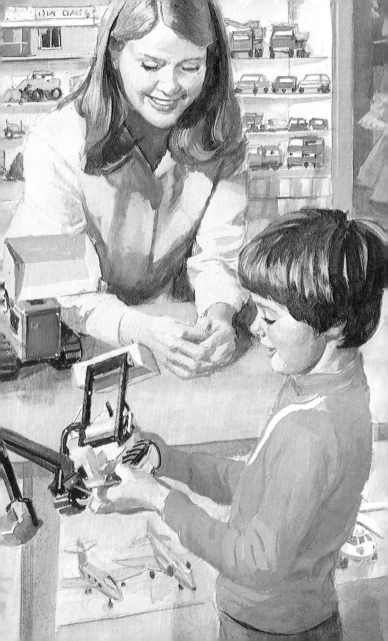

Jane is in

the toy shop

The dog is in the toy shop.

Peter has a toy

and

Jane has a toy

---

new word

has

Peter has a ball

Peter likes

the ball.

---

new word   ball

Here is the dog.

The dog has

the ball.

Here is a tree.

The ball is in

the tree.

---

new word

tree

Peter is in the tree and Jane is in the tree.

---

no new words

Here is Peter

in the tree.

Peter has

the ball.

New words used in this book

Total number of new words: 16
Average repetition per word: 10